FOUR GIRLS AND A COMPACT

BY

ANNIE HAMILTON DONNELL

Four Girls And A Compact

CHAPTER I.

"Wait for T.O.," commanded Loraine, and of course they waited. Loraine's commands were always obeyed, Laura Ann said, because her name was such a queeny one. Nobody else in the little colony—the "B-Hive"—had a queeny name.

"Though I just missed it," sighed Laura Ann. "Think what a little step from Loraine to Laur' Ann! I always just miss things."

T.O. was apt to be late. She never rode, and, being short, was not a remarkable walker. To-night she was later than usual. The three other girls got into kimonos and slippers and prepared tea. In all their minds the Grand Plan was fomenting, and it was not easy to wait. A cheer greeted T.O. as she came in, wct and weary and cheerful.

"You're overdue, my dear," Loraine said severely. But of course T.O. laughed and offered a weak pun:

"The 'dew' is over me, you mean! Oh, girls, this looks too cozy for anything in here! All the way up town I've been blessing you three for taking me in."

Said Laura Ann: "If I were pun-mad, like some folks, I could do something quite smart there. But there, you poor, wet dear! You sha'n't be outdone in your specialty, no you sha'n't! Get off your things quick, dear—we're all bursting to talk about the Grand Plan."

It was, after all, Billy that started in. Billy was very tired indeed, and her lean, eager face was pale.

"Girls, we must!" she said. "I can't hold out more than a few weeks more. I shall be a mental wreck and go 'round muttering, one-two—three—four, one—two—three—four—flat your b's, sharp your c's—one—two—three—four—play!" For Billy all day toiled at pianos, teaching unwilling little persons to play. Billy's long name was Wilhelmina.

They were all toilers—worker-B's. The "B" part of the name which they had given to the little colony came from the accident of all their surnames beginning with that letter—Brown, Bent, Baker, Byers. It was, they all agreed, a happy accident; the "B-Hive" sounded so well. But, as Laura Ann said, it entailed things, notably industry.

Laura Ann finished negatives part of the day to earn money to learn to paint the other part. She was poor, but the same good grit that made her loyal to her old grandmother's name, unshortened and unbeautified, gave her courage to work on toward the distant goal.

Loraine taught—"just everlastingly taught," she said, until she could do it with her eyes shut. Cube root, all historic dates, all x, y, z's, were as printing to her, dinned into the warp and woof of her by patient reiteration. She was very tired, too. The rest of the long June days stretched ahead of her in weary perspective.

That these three had drifted together in the great city was sufficiently curious, but more curious yet was the "drifting together" of T.O.—a plain little clerk in a great department store. She, herself, humbly acknowledged that she did not seem to "belong," but here she was, divesting herself of her wet wraps and getting ready for tea in the tiny flat. Handkerchiefs, initialed, "warranted,"—uninitialed, unwarranted—were behind her and ahead, but between she forgot their existence and took her comfort.

"Well?" she said presently. "I'm ready." They sat down to the simple little meal without further delay and with the first mouthfuls opened again the rather time-worn discussion. Could they adopt the Grand Plan? Oh, couldn't they? To get out of the hot, teeming city and breathe air enough and pure enough, to luxuriate in idleness, to rest—to a girl, they longed for it. They were all orphans, and they were all poor. The Grand Plan was ambitious, indefinite, but they could not give it up. They had wintered it and springed it, and clung to it through bright days and dark.

Suddenly Loraine tapped sharply on the table. "All in favor of spending the summer in the country say 'aye,'" she cried, "and say it hard!"

"Aye!"

"Aye!"

"Aye!"

"Aye!" appended Loraine, and said it hard. "It's a vote," she added calmly. Then, staring at each other, they sat for a little with rather frightened faces. For this thing that they had done was rather a stupendous thing. T.O. recovered first—courage was as the breath of her little lean nostrils.

"Girls, this is great!" she laughed. "We've gone and done it! There's nothing left but to pack our trunks!"

"Except a few last trifles, such as deciding where to go and what to pay for it with," put in Laura Ann with soft irony. "We could decide those things on the train, I suppose—"

"Let's decide 'em on the spot," rejoined T.O. imperturbably. "Somebody propose something."

Here Billy was visited with one of her inspirations and promptly shared it with her usual generosity. "We must hunt up a place to—er—'bunk' in—just bunk and board ourselves. Of course we can't afford to be boarded—"

"Of course," in chorus.

"Well, then, one of us must go out into the waste places—oh, anywhere where the grass has room to grow and there are trees and birds and barns—I stipulate barns." Billy made a splendid, comprehensive gesture that took in all the points of the compass impartially. "One of us must take a few days off and go and hunt up a nice, inexpensive little Eldorado for us. There!—there, my friends, you have the solution of your knotty little problem in a nutshell. I gladly give my 'services' free."

"Who's going?" demanded practical Laura Ann. "Does anybody kindly volunteer?"

No volunteers. Silence, broken only by the chirp of the cheery little teakettle. The immense responsibility of setting the Grand Plan in motion was not to be lightly assumed. The utter vagueness of Billy's "waste places" was dismaying, to say the least. There might be many nice, inexpensive little Eldorados waiting to be "bunked" in and picnicked in, but where? The world was full of places where there were trees and birds and barns, but to pick out the particular one where four tired-out young toilers could lay down their tools and restinexpensively, looked like a big undertaking.

Billy had settled back in her chair with an air of having done her part and washed her hands of further responsibility. The rest must do their parts now. Billy, who was the youngest and frailest of the little colony of workers, had fallen into the way of dropping asleep whenever opportunity offered; she did so now with a little sigh of contentment. Her girlish face against the faded crimson back of the chair looked startlingly white. In her sleep she moved her lips and the others caught a pathetic little "one-two-three-four" dropping from them. Poor Billy! She was giving a music lesson in her dreams!

Loraine made a little paper shade and shielded her pale face from the light, and Laura Ann tilted the clumsy patent rocker backward and trigged it with a book. Both their faces, tired, too, and pale, were sweet with kindness. T.O., who did queer and unexpected things, went round the table on her toes and kissed Billy's forehead openly. Her face had a puckering frown on it, oddly at variance with the kiss and with the look in her eyes. The kiss and the look were the things that mattered—the frown was a thing of insignificance.

"You poor little blessed!" she murmured.

"'Flat your b,'" murmured Billy wearily, and no one laughed. They were all laughers, but the picture of Billy toiling on monotonously in her sleep failed to appeal to them as humorous. T.O. went back silently to her seat.

What the initials T.O. stood for in the way of a name had been the subject of much guessing in the B-Hive, for the owner of the initials refused whimsically to explain them. Perhaps she would sometime when the moon was full or the wind was in the right quarter, she said. Meanwhile T.O. did well enough—as well as "Billy," anyway, or "Laura Ann"! And they fell in gayly with her whimsy and called her T.O. The nearest they had ever come to an answer to their guesses was one night when they had been discussing "talents" and comparing "callings," and T.O. had sat by, a wistful little listener and admirer. For T.O. had no talent, and who would call selling handkerchiefs from morning till night a "calling"? Even sheer, fine handkerchiefs, warranted every thread linen!

"Talentless One," she broke out startlingly. "You want to know what 'T.O.' stands for—that's it!" And the amused look in the girls' eyes changed quickly to understanding at sight of her face. "Well," she challenged, "why don't you say what an appropriate name it is? It's a wonder you talented ones didn't guess it long ago! Listen! Loraine's talent is writing—we all know she'll be an author some day. Laura Ann's is art. Oh, you needn't laugh—need she, girls? One of these days we're all going to a 'hanging,' and it'll be Laura Ann's! Billy's talent everybody knows. She can play wicked folks good, if there's a piano handy. Well, what is my talent? Don't everybody speak at once!" The girl's flushed face defied them. It was bitter with longing to be a Talented One.

"Dear!" It was like gentle Loraine to begin with a "dear," and like her, too, to cross the room to T.O. and touch her little bitter face with cool fingers. "Dear, don't you worry—your talent is there."

"Where?" demanded T.O. Then she laughed. "I suppose you mean buried in a handkerchief! But I shall never be able to dig it out—never! There's such an awful pile of them on top! They keep piling on new ones every day. If I keep on selling handkerchiefs till I'm seventy-five, I'll never get down to my talent."

It was, after all, quite true, though none of them would acknowledge it—except the Talentless One herself. She was, as she insisted, the odd one in the busy little B-Hive. Her very face, small and dark and lean, was an "odd" one; the faces of the other three were marked by an indefinable something that she called talent, and she was not far wrong. A subtle refinement, intellectuality, asserted itself gently in all three of them. The dark little face of T.O. was vivacious and keen, but not refined or intellectual.

Billy was the baby "B," as Loraine was the acknowledged queen. They all favored Billy and took care of her. Was it a rainy morning? Somebody got Billy's rubbers, somebody else her umbrella! Was the child paler than usual? She must have the softest chair and be babied. Poor little toiler-Billy, created to have a mother and a home, to sit always in soft chairs and be taken care of! Yet without them all she was making a splendid struggle for independence, with the best of them, and they were conscious of a certain element of heroism in her toiling that none of the rest of them laid claim to in their own. The other B.'s were proud of Billy.

T.O. was as small and thin as Billy, but no one thought of taking care of T.O. or babying her. Instead, T.O.—the Talentless One—took care of them all. She had always been a toiler, always been alone, and to the rest it was comparatively a new experience. T.O., as she herself said, was able to give them all "points."

While tired Billy slept to-night, the Grand Plan discussion was taken up again and entertained with new enthusiasm. It was now a definite Plan, since they had voted unanimously to adopt it—it was no longer merely a unanimous wish, to be bandied about longingly. It remained only to choose a brave soul to go forth and find for it a "local habitation."

"When Billy wakes up, we'll draw lots," Loraine decided gently. "The one who gets the longest slip will go—but mercy! I hope I sha'n't be the one! Girls, there really ought to be one to—er—oversee the drawing of the lots—"

"Hear! Hear!" from T.O.

"You will take your chances with the common herd, my dear," Laura Ann said firmly. "You really need not be alarmed, though, for I shall draw the fatal slip. I always do. Then I shall go up-country and engage four boards at a nice white house with green blinds, and forget to ask how much they will cost—the 'boards,' I mean—and whether they'll take Billy at half-price. You'll all like my white house, but you won't be able to stay more than one night on account of the expense. So you'll turn me out of the B-Hive and I shall—"

"Oh, don't do anything else—don't!" T.O. groaned. "That will be doing enough."

"We shall have to find a very cheap place," Loraine said, thoughtfully, too intent on the fate of the Grand Plan to listen to pleasantries. "Somewhere where it won't cost much of anything."

"Such an easy place to find!" murmured Laura Ann. "I see myself going straight to it!"

"We've got to go to it, on account of—" Loraine nodded toward the sleeping little figure in the softest chair. "Girls, Billy is all worn out."

"So are you," Laura Ann said tenderly.

"And you," retorted Loraine.

The Talentless One, unintentionally left out, sighed an infinitesimal sigh, preparatory to smiling stoutly.

"Of course we're going to find the right place," she said convincingly. "You wait and see. I see it now"—this dreamily; it was odd for the Talentless One to be dreaming. "It looks this way: Green, grassy and pine-woodsy and roomy. And cornfields—think of it!"

"'Woods and cornfields—the picture must not be over-done,'" quoted softly and a little accusingly Laura Ann. But the Talentless One had never heard of Miss Cary's beautiful poem, and went on calmly:

"And a—pump. Girls, if I find the 'Eldorado,' there'll be a pump—painted blue!"

Here Billy woke up. There was no time to discountenance the pump.

"Why, I believe I've been asleep!" Billy laughed restedly. "And I've been somewhere else, too. Guess!"

"To Eldorado," someone ventured.

"Well, I have. It was the loveliest place! There weren't any pianos or schools or photograph salons or handkerchiefs in it!"

"Then we'll go there!" the Talentless One cried.

Loraine was busy cutting strips of paper. She cut four of varying lengths and dropped them into an empty cracker-box.

"Somebody shake them up, everyone shut her eyes and draw one," she ordered. "And the person that draws the longest slip must be the one to find our Eldorado."

They shut their eyes and fumbled in the cracker-box. The room was oddly quiet. Laura Ann, who always drew the fatal slip, breathed a little hard.

But the lot fell to the Talentless One.

CHAPTER II.

"Why, I didn't get it!" exclaimed Laura Ann, in surprise. "And maybe I'm not thankful! Poor T.O.!"

"Yes, poor T.O.!" agreed Loraine and Billy. The honor of drawing the longest slip was not, it appeared, a coveted one. But T.O. actually beamed!

"Needn't anyone pity me!" she said, briskly. "I like it! You see," she added, explanatorily, "I never did anything remarkable before! Of course I sha'n't blame you girls any if you shake in your shoes while I'm gone, but I'll promise to do my little best. If you thought you could trust me—"

"We do! We do!" Loraine said, warmly, speaking for them all. "And we pity you, too, poor dear! It looks like an awful undertaking to me."

"How long can you take? Are you sure they'll let you get off down at Torrey's?" asked Billy, languidly.

"Oh," the Talentless One said, calmly, "I shall get a substitute, of course. They let the girls do that, if the substitute suits 'em. There's a girl that used to be at the handkerchief counter that will be glad enough to earn a little money, I know. She'll be tickled! And she can keep the place open for me when I get back from the country in the fall—" Suddenly the Talentless One laughed out joyously. "Hear me! 'When I get back from the country!' Doesn't that sound splendid! Makes me think of cows and chickens and strawberries and—"

"Pumps painted blue!" laughed Laura Ann. "We're in for a blue pump, girls!"

The substitution at the handkerchief counter could not be arranged for at once, so the proposed voyage of discovery was a little delayed. Meanwhile the Grand Plan and a newly-born family of lesser plans occupied the interim of waiting. One thing they all agreed upon. It was tired little Billy who voiced it.

"We won't be good this summer, will we? I've been good so long that I want to rest!"

"It would seem comfortable not to have to be, wouldn't it?" Loraine laughed. As if Loraine could rest from being good! "Not to have to do anything for anybody—just be good to yourself! Now, I call that the luxury of selfishness! And really, girls, we deserve one little luxury—"

"We'll indulge ourselves," T.O. nodded gravely. "I'm sure I've been polite to people and patient with people long enough to have a vacation—a summer vacation!"

"Give me a paper and pencil, somebody, quick!" This from Laura Ann. She fell to scribbling industriously. The purring of her pencil over the paper had a smooth, wicked sound as if it were writing wicked things. It was.

"Be it known," read Laura Ann, flourishing her pencil, "that we, the undersigned, having endeavored, up to the present, to be good, consider ourselves entitled to be selfish during our summer vacation. That we mean to be selfish—that we herewith swear to be! That we do not mean to 'do good unto' anybody except ourselves! Inasmuch as we have faithfully tried to do our several duties hitherto, we feel justified in resting from the same until such time as we may—er—wish to begin again.

"Furthermore, resolved: That any or all persons hereunto subscribed, who fail to keep the letter of this compact, be summarily dropped!"

(Signed) "LAURA ANN BYERS."

The paper went the rounds and was soberly signed by each girl in turn. Loraine, the last, traced three words in her tiny handwriting at the head of the paper.

"The Wicked Compact!" read Billy over her shoulder, and nodded agreeingly. "That's a good name for it. Doesn't it make you feel lovely and shuddery to belong to a Wicked Compact! Oh, you needn't think I shall go back on the rules and regulations! If somebody gets down on his knees and implores, 'Which note shall I flat?' I shall turn coldly away, or else say, 'Suit yourself, my dear!' But, girls, oh girls, I hope there won't be any pianos in Eldorado!"

"Probably there will be only cabinet organs—don't worry, dear!" soothed Laura Ann.

The day after the Wicked Compact was drawn up and signed, T.O. started on her quest for Eldorado. She would have no one escort her to the station; she would give no intimation of her plans. They were all to wait as patiently as possible till she came back. It was only because she had to, poor child, that she accepted the contributions of the others toward her expenses of travel.

At the station she straightened her short stature to its utmost and approached the ticket window. She might have been, from her splendid dignity of manner, six feet instead of five.

"Will you please tell me which road is the cheapest to travel on?" she asked, clearly, undismayed outwardly, inwardly quailing before the ticket man's amazement. His curious eyes surveyed her through the little opening.

"Why—er—well, there's the most competition on the X & Y Road," he said, slowly. "The rates on that line are about down to the limit—"

"Thank you," the dignified one said, and turned away. She found the time table of the X & Y Road on the station wall, and studied it thoughtfully. She had resolved to select the place with the most promising name. Back at the ticket window she patiently waited her turn in a little stream of people. The woman ahead of her was flourishing a dainty, embroidered handkerchief, and she wondered idly if it had come from her counter at Torrey's. If so, why was it not a little white flag of truce that gave her a right to say "How do you do?" to the woman? The Talentless One suddenly felt a little lonely.

"Ticket to Placid Pond, please," she said, when her turn came. The very sound of the peaceful little name gave her courage. Placid Pond! Placid Pond! Could any place be more indicative of rest? Then she bethought her of the Wicked Compact, and felt almost impelled to hand back the ticket—Placid Pond could not be the right place to be bad in!

But it was too late!

"Two-twenty," the ticket man said, monotonously, and she fumbled in her lean, little purse. To Placid Pond she would go, and, if there were barns and cornfields and a blue-painted pump—the thrill of expectancy ran through her veins, and she forgot the Wicked Compact.

The Talentless One had never glided through green places like this before, between slow, clear little streams, by country children waving their hats. She had never seen far, splendid reaches of hills, undulating softly against the sky. Wonder and delight filled her. She found herself envying the little, brown children who waved their hats.

"It's pretty, ain't it?" a fresh, old voice said in her ear. When she turned, it was to look into a fresh, old face behind her.

"Ain't it a pretty world the Lord's made? The 'firmament showeth his handiwork,' don't it? Where are you going to, deary?"

"A place called Placid Pond," answered the girl, smiling back.

"No? Well, I declare! That's where Emmeline Camp lives that was a Jones an' spelt out o' my spellin'-book! If you see Emmeline, you tell her you saw me on the cars. Emmeline and I have always kep' up our interest in each other. She'll be tickled—you tell her I've learnt that leaf-stitch at last! She'll understand!"

The thin, old voice tinkled on pleasantly in the Talentless One's ears.

"Come back here an' set with me, deary, an' I'll tell you which house is Emmeline's, so, if you go past, you'll know it—it's painted green! Did you ever! But Emmeline was always set on green. She was married in a green silk, an' we girls said she married a green husband!"

T.O. laughed enjoyingly. She began to feel acquainted with Emmeline, and to hope she should find the green house—perhaps it would be the Eldorado house! Wonders happened sometimes.

"I don't suppose—there isn't a blue pump, is there? I've set my heart on a blue pump!" she laughed, as if the little, old woman who knew Emmeline would understand. The little, old woman smiled delightedly—as if she understood!

"Dear land, no! I hope Emmeline ain't painted her pump blue—and her livin' in a green house! But she'd go out an' do it—it would be just like Emmeline, if she knew anybody wanted a blue pump! Here we are, deary! This is Placid Pond we're coming to! You see that sheet o' water, don't you? Well, that's it!"

The Talentless One buttoned her jacket and clutched her little black bag. Her thin cheeks bloomed suddenly with tiny red spots of excitement. She seemed on the edge of an Adventure; and, to one who had stood behind a counter nearly all her days, an Adventure began with a capital A. The train slowed up and stood panting—in a hurry to go again.

"Oh, I wish you were going to get out here!" T.O. said, wistfully.

The little, old woman seemed like an old friend to her. She felt oddly young and inexperienced. Then, remembering the girls left behind in the B-Hive and their confidence in her, she threw up her small head and hurried away valiantly.

"Good-by!" she called back, from the bit of platform outside.

"Good-by! Give my love to Emmeline!" nodded and beamed the little, old face in the car window.

It was a tiny place. T.O. could see only the great, placid sheet of water and the diminutive station at first. She accosted the only human being in sight.

"Which way is the city—village, I mean?" she asked.

He was an old man and held a scooped palm behind his ear.

"Eh?"

"The village—please direct me to it."

"Well," he laughed good-humoredly, "all the village they is you'll strike yonder," pointing. "You keep a-goin', an' you'll git thar!"

She thanked him and set out courageously. She kept "a-goin'." The country road was shady and dusty and sweet with mystic, unseen, growing things. Her feet, used to hard pavements, sank into the soft dust luxuriously. She breathed deep and swung along at a splendid pace. It was hard to believe that she was a clerk at Torrey's! There did not seem to have ever been handkerchiefs in the world—even all-linen, warranted ones!

"This is Eldorado!" she said aloud, and was proud of herself for finding it so soon—coming straight to it! Lucky she had been the one to draw the longest strip.

She passed one or two houses, but none of them were painted green. She said to herself she would keep on to "Emmeline's" house. The whim had seized her and was holding on tight that Emmeline's might be the Right Place. So she swung on buoyantly.

A stone wall bordered the road on one side, and over the wall she spied a sprinkling of little flowers that called, "Come and pick us!" to her. She did not know that they were bluets, but she knew they were dainty and sweet and beckoned to her. She paused an instant uncertainly, and then climbed the wall. It was rather an arduous undertaking for a clerk at a handkerchief counter, and she went about it clumsily. The wall was high and the stones "jiggled" in a terrifying way. One big stone climbed down on the other side with her—they went together unceremoniously.

The Talentless One laughed a little under her breath as she sat up among the little flowers, but she was not quite sure that she wanted to laugh. The big stone was on her foot and she regarded it with disfavor. It required considerable strength to roll it off—then she got up. Then she sank down again very suddenly.

"Oh!" she cried, sharply. For several moments she said nothing more, did nothing more. The discovery she had made was not a pleasant discovery. In Eldorado clumsy people who could not climb stone walls came to grief. She had come to grief. When she moved her foot, terrible twinges of pain were telegraphed all over her body. She sat, a sorry little heap, among the stranger flowers that had brought about her ruin. The roadway stretched dustily and emptily up and down, on the other side of the wall.

"Oh!" breathed the Talentless One. It had been a sigh before, now it was a groan. What was she to do? A sort of terror seized her. She had never been really frightened before. The beautiful country about her no longer was beautiful. It was no longer Eldorado to her.

Then she discovered a green fleck down the road, a different green from the grass and trees. If it should be Emmeline's house—if she could get to it!

"I must!" she said, and hobbled to her feet. Somehow she got over the wall, and went stumbling toward the green spot. The agony in her foot increased every moment; she grew dizzy with it.

It must be Emmeline's house—a little, green-painted one beside the road! There could not be two green houses in Placid Pond. With a long breath of relief she got to the door. After that she did not know anything for a little time, then her eyes opened. Someone with a kind, anxious face was bending over her. It was Emmeline! It looked like the face of an old friend to the poor, little Talentless One.

"There, there, poor dear! Never mind where you be, or who I be—you 'tend right to gettin' out o' your faint! Sniff this bottle—there! You'll be all right in a minute. It's your foot, ain't it? It's all swollen up—how'd you sprain it?"

She had the injured foot in her tremulous old hands, gently loosening the shoe. The girl, though she winced with pain, did not utter a sound.

"There ain't any doctor this side of Anywhere," the kind voice ran on, "but never you mind. I'll risk but what I've got liniments that will doctor you up."

And the girl, looking up into the peaceful old "lineaments," smiled faintly, and knew there was healing in them. Even in her throbbing pain she could think of this new pun that she would regale the girls with when she got back to them—if she ever got back!

"You are 'Emmeline,' aren't you!" she presently questioned, feebly, like an old woman, for the pain seemed to have made her old. "I'm so glad you are Emmeline!"

Poor dear, she was wandering in her mind, and no wonder, with a foot swollen up like that! It was queer, though, hitting on the right name in that way.

"There! there! Yes, I am Emmeline, though I might've been Sophia or Debby Jane! Namin' people is sort o' accidental. I always wished they'd named me somethin' prettier by accident! But I guess Emmeline will have to do."

It was long after this before any explanation was made. The fact that it was Emmeline was enough for those first hours.

"Now, you kind of bear on to yourself, poor dear! This boot has got to come off!" the kind voice crooned. But, in the awful process of "bearing on," the Talentless One shot out into the dark, as if pushed by a heavy hand. How long it was before she came back into the light she did not know—it seemed to be a point of light that pricked her eyes. She shut them against it, and longed to drift away again; the dark had been cool and pleasant.

It was a lighted lamp on a tiny, round table. She found it out the next time she opened her eyes. She was in a little bedroom, on the bed. The door was open, and a voice drifted in to her:

"She was coming to beautifully when I left her. I thought mebbe she'd feel more at home to come to alone. I've got her ankle all dressed nice, but it would make your heart ache to see it! The poor dear won't walk again this one while—"

"But, Emmeline Camp, what are you going to do with her all that time?" The second voice was a little shrill.

"Sh! I'm goin' to doctor her up, just as if she was the little girl the Lord never gave me. I've always known what I'd do if my little girl broke anything—There! you'll have to excuse me, Mrs. Williams, while I take this cup o'tea in."

It is odd how many little confidences can be exchanged in the time of cooling and drinking a cup of tea. The caller had gone away, and the old woman and the girl were left alone. Little by little the story of the B-Hive and the quest for an Eldorado came out. Emmeline Camp sat and nodded, and clandestinely wiped her eyes.

"I see—I see, deary! Now, don't you talk any more and get faint again. I'll talk. You no need to worry about anything in the world—not yet! When it's time to commence, I'll tell you. How does your foot feel now? Dear, dear! When I was fussing over it, it seemed just as if it was my little Amelia's foot! I've always known what I'd do if she sprained hers, and so I did it to yours, deary!"

"Is Amelia your daughter?"

The old face wavered between a smile and tears. "Yes," she nodded, "but she warn't ever born. It's a kind of a secret between me and the Lord. He knows I've made believe Amelia. I've always been kind of lonesome, an' she's been a sight of company to me. She's been a good daughter, Amelia has!" Now it was a smile. "We've set an' sewed patchwork together, ever since she grew up. When she was little—there, deary, hear me run on! But you remind me so much of Amelia. You can laugh just as much as you want to at me runnin' on like this about a little girl that warn't ever born—mebbe laughin' will help your foot."

She took up the empty cup and went away, but she came back and stood a minute in the doorway.

"There's this about it," she laughed, in a tender, little way, "if she warn't ever born, she won't ever die. I sha'n't lose Amelia!"

To the three girls waiting at the B-Hive came a letter. They read it, three heads in a bunch:

"Eldorado, June 26.

"Come whenever you want to. Directions enclosed."

CHAPTER III.

There was a postscript. It was like T.O. to put the most of the letter into the postscript.

"P.S.—Never call me the Talentless One again" (as if they ever had!), "when I came straight to the Eldorado—tumbled right into it. I've decided to stay here until you come—please tell my substitute so. I know she'll be so glad she'll throw up her hat. Bring your sheets and pillow-cases. Come by way of the X. & Y. R.R. to a place called Placid Pond."

The three readers, bunched together over the letter, uttered a cry of delight. "Placid Pond!"— of all the dear, delightful, placid names! The very look of it on paper was restful; itsounded restful when you said it over and over—"Placid Pond. Placid Pond. Placid Pond."

"Oh, she's a dear—she's an artist!" cried Laura Ann, who measured all things by their relationship to art. This was an own cousin!

"Read on—somebody hold the letter still!" Billy cried excitedly. And they read on: "Take the only road there is to take, and keep on to a house that's painted green. It will be Emmeline's house, though they might have named her Sophia, she says, by accident. But you will be glad she is Emmeline. She has a beautiful daughter that never was born and never will die—oh, girls, come as quick as ever you can!"

Yours, "The Talented One."

"P.S. No. 2.—Don't climb any stone walls. The stones are not stuck on."

For a tiny space the three girls looked at each other in silence. The letter in Loraine's hand was a masterpiece, full of enticing mysteries that beckoned to them to come and find the "answers." What kind of an Eldorado was this that was called Placid Pond, and was full of mysteries? How could they wait! They must pack up and go at once!

"'Talented One,' indeed!—she's a genius! See how she's left us to guess things, instead of explaining them all out in a nice, tame way—oh, girls"—Laura Ann's eyes shone—"won't we have the greatest time!"

"What I want to know is, who is Emmeline—"

"Yes, who is Emmeline?" "And who can her daughter be? She sounds so lovely and ghostly!"

"Everything sounds lovely and ghostly. When can we go, girls?" This from practical Loraine. "I can't till after the Fourth."

"Nor I," groaned Billy, dolefully.

"I could, but I shall not—I shall wait for you two," Laura Ann said quietly.

Loraine turned upon her. "You needn't," she said, "now that you've signed the compact—you can do whatever you want to now, you know. Needn't think of anybody but yourself."

"The privilege of being selfish doesn't begin till we get to Eldorado," laughed Laura Ann. "You'll see what I do then!"

It was arranged that they should start on the fifth of July. "With our sheets and pillow-cases," appended Billy. No one thought of writing to T.O. for further particulars. No one wanted further particulars. The uncertainly and mystery that enveloped Eldorado was its greatest charm. They speculated, to be sure, at odd moments, as to the identity of the person who might have been Sophia but was Emmeline, and they wrestled a little with the hidden meaning of Postscript Number Two. Why were they especially bidden not to climb stone walls? And why was the Talented One "staying over" till they came?

"Why? Why? Why?" chanted Billy, "but don't anybody dare to guess why! Who wants to know!"

"Not me!" echoed ungrammatically Laura Ann.

While they waited and speculated mildly, and packed and repacked their things, T.O. lay on the bed in Emmeline Camp's little bedroom and winced with pain whenever she moved her wounded foot. But she was very happy. "Peace is in my soul, if not my sole!" she thought, a slave still to the punning habit. She had never been so peaceful in her life. The little old woman who had befriended her bustled happily in and out of the little bedroom. She bathed and rubbed the swollen ankle, and smiled and chattered to the girl at the other end of it. Her "lineaments" were working a cure, surely.

It had all been decided upon. The B-Hive was to be transplanted for the summer to the little, green-painted house trailed over with morning-glory vines and roses. Emmeline Camp had wanted, she said, for forty years, to go upon a long journey, to visit her brother. Here was her chance. The small sum she had at last consented to be paid for the use of her little house would pay her traveling expenses one way, at least, and John would be glad enough, she said, to pay her fare home, to get rid of her! Only she was quite able to pay it herself.

"I've kind of hankered to go to see John all these years. Forty years is quite a spell to hanker, isn't it? But I never felt like leaving the house behind, and I couldn't take it along very conveniently, so I stayed to home. And then—my dear, you can laugh as well as not, but I didn't like to leave Amelia."

"But you might have taken her with—"

"No," seriously, "I couldn't 've taken Amelia. I think, deary, it might 've killed her; she's part of the little house and the morning-glories and roses. I'd have had to leave Amelia if I'd gone, and it didn't seem right."

"But now—"

"Now," the little, old woman laughed in her odd, tender way that "went with" Amelia, "now she'll have plenty of young company—all o' you here with her. I shall make believe she's coming and going with you, and it'll be a sight of comfort. Yes, deary, I guess this is going to be my chance to visit John."

"And our chance to have a summer in the country," completed the Talented One. "Oh, I think you are—dear! Whatever will the other girls say when I tell them about you!"

One day T.O. remembered the blue pump. She gazed out of the window at the brown one in the little yard. "Who would have thought," she sighed, "that I could be so happy without a blue pump!"

"What's that, deary?" The little, old woman was sewing patchwork near by.

"Oh," laughed the girl, "I always did want a pump that was painted blue. I saw a picture of one once when I was a little mite, and it impressed me—such a lovely, bright blue! I thought it went beautifully with the green grass! But I can get along without it, I guess."

"We have to get along without having things painted to suit us," nodded the little, old woman philosophically. But she remembered the blue pump. There was a can of paint out in the shed room, and there was Jane Cotton's Sam.

Jane Cotton's Sam was a "feature" of Placid Pond—a whole set of features, T.O. said. He was a lumbering, awkward fellow, well up to the end of his teens, the only hope of widowed Jane. The Lord had given him a splendid head, but the Placid Pond people were secretly triumphing in the knowledge that Sam had failed to pass in his college examinations, "head or no head." Jane had always boasted so of Sam's brains, and predicted such a wonderful future for him! All her soul was set on Sam's success—well, wasn't it time her pride had a fall? Mebbe now she'd see Sam wasn't much different from other people's boys.

Jane's heart was reported to be broken by the boy's failure, and Sam went about sulkily defiant. He made a great pretense of lofty indifference, but maybe he didn't care!—maybe not! Emmeline Camp knew in her gentle old heart that he cared. She worried about Sam.

All this the Talented One learned, little by little, in the way country gossip is learned. She learned many other things, too, about the neighbors—things that she lay and pondered about. It seemed queer to find out that even a placid little place like this, set among the peaceful hills, had its tragedies and comedies—its pitiful little skeletons behind the doors.

"That's Old '61," Mrs. Camp said, pointing to an old figure in the road. "See him go marching past!—he always marches, as if he heard drums beating and he was keeping time. I tell 'em he does hear 'em. He lives all alone up on the edge o' the woods, and folks say he spends most all his time trying to pick march tunes out on the organ. A few years ago he got some back pension money, and up and spent it for a cabinet organ! Dear land! it seemed a pity, when he might have got him some nice clothes or something sensible. But there he sets and sets over that organ, trying to pick out tunes! Well,"—the gentle old voice took on charity— "well, if that's his way of being happy, I s'pose he's got as good a right to it as I have to— Amelia," a whimsical little smile lighting up the old face, but underlying it the tenderness that the girl on the bed had come to look for whenever any reference was made to Amelia.

"We've all got our idiosyncreases," added Emmeline Camp, "only some of 'em's creased in a little deeper'n others. I guess mine and Old '61's are pretty considerable deep!"

The early July days were cloudless and full of hot, stinging noises. T.O. crawled out to lie in the grass under a great tree, and exult in room and freedom and rest. Her ankle was still very painful, but she regarded it with philosophical toleration: "You needn't have climbed a stone wall, need you? Well, then, what have you to complain of? The best thing you can do is to keep still." Which was, without doubt, the truth. "Anyhow, it isn't becoming in you to be so puffed up!"

It was decided that Mrs. Camp should start on her trip before the other girls arrived. Hence, on the morning of the day they had set to come, the little old woman and her bags and bundles rode away down the dusty country road. Her lean, brown, crumpled old face had an exalted expression; the joy of anticipation and the triumph of patient waiting met in it and blended oddly. It was a great day for Emmeline Camp.

"Good-by, deary. Keep right on rubbing, and don't go to walking 'round. There's some cookies left in the cooky-crock, and a pie or two on the shelf to kind of set you going. Take good care o' yourselves."

"And Amelia," whispered the girl, drawing the old face down to her. "We'll take good care of Amelia."

It was a little lonely after the old stage rumbled away. The Talented One turned whimsically to Amelia for company. She tried to imagine her, as the little old woman did, but in vain. She could not conjure up the sweet, elusive face, the hair, the eyes, the grave little mouth of Amelia. The little old woman had taken away with her love, the key. She must have taken Amelia away with her, too, the girl thought, smiling at her own fancy. So, for company, she must wait until Loraine and Billy and Laura Ann came, on the further edge of the day. She lay in the cool grass, and made beatific plans for all the long, lazy days to come. No hurrying, or worrying—each one for herself, happy in her own way. Only themselves to think of for the space of a golden summer!

"I am glad she took Amelia," the girl in the grass laughed softly. "We'd never be able to keep to the Compact with Amelia 'round—Amelia would never have signed a 'Wicked Compact'!" Which, in the event of gentle, unsinning Amelia ever having been born, might or might not have been true. It would have been harder work, reflected the girl in the grass, for Amelia to have been unsinning and gentle, if she had been born.

Jane Cotton's Sam came lounging down the road, cap over one eye, face surlily defiant. T.O. watched him with displeasure. So that was the kind of a boy that gave up? Poor kind of a boy! Why didn't he try it again, especially when his poor mother's heart was breaking? Didn't he know that giving up was worse than failing in his examinations? Somebody ought to tell him—why, he was stopping at Mrs. Camp's little front gate! He was coming in!

The girl lying in the long grass under the tree sat up hurriedly. Quick, quick! what was his name? Oh, yes, Sam!

"Good-morning, Sam," she said pleasantly. But the boy, with a mere nod of his splendidly-modeled head, hurried away toward the tiny barn. The girl had seen the dark flush that mounted upward from his neck over his pink and white cheeks.

"Poor thing! He knows I know that he didn't pass—that is the only 'out' about living in the country: everybody knows everything. Well, if it makes him blush, then his mother needn't break her heart yet. I like the looks of that boy, if he does go 'round scowling." Whereupon the Talented One promptly dismissed Jane Cotton's Sam from her meditations. It did not occur to her to question his right to be on Mrs. Camp's premises. She lay back in the grass and took up again the interrupted thread of her musings. By gentle degrees odd fancies took possession of her.

The sprinkling of great, white daisies in the grass beside her—suppose, now, this minute, they changed into white handkerchiefs, spread out on a green counter! Then she would have to sell them to passers-by; it was her business to sell handkerchiefs. Someone was coming marching up the road—suppose she tried to sell him one, for the fun of it!—to make a good story for the girls. Laughing, she got up and leaned on the fence. She "dared" herself to do it. Then, courteously, "Can I sell you anything in handkerchiefs to-day? Initialed, embroidered—"

The marching feet stopped. Shrewd old eyes studied her face and twinkled, responsive to the harmless mischief visible in it.

"You got any with flags on—in the corners or anywhere? Or drums on?" It was Old '61. "Or red, white an' blue ones? I'd like one o' them—I fit in the war," explanatorily.

"Yes?" The saleswoman was not especially interested in the war; it is not the way with many of her kind to be interested in things.

"I fit clear through—in the Wilderness, and Bull Run, an' plenty more. They couldn't get rid o' me, the enemy couldn't! No, sir, where there was marchin' an' shootin', I was bound to be there! They hit me time 'n' again, but I didn't waste no unnecessary time in hospittles—I had to git back to the boys."

She was interested now; she forgot she was to sell him a handkerchief. "Go on," she said.

"It was great! You ought to heard the drums an' smelt the smoke, an' felt your feet marchin' under you, an' your knapsack poundin' your back—yes, sir, an' bein' hungry an' thirsty an' wore out! You'd ought to seen how ragged the boys got, an' heard 'em whistlin' 'Through Georgy' while they sewed on patches—oh, you'd ought to whistled 'Through Georgy'!"

The girl, watching the kindled old face, saw a shadow creep over it.

"I useter—I useter—but someway I've lost it. It's pretty hard to've marched through Georgy an' forgot the tune about. Some days I 'most get holt of it again—I thought I could, on the organ, but I can't, not the hull of it. Someway I've lost it—it's pretty hard. It ha'nts me—if you ever be'n ha'nted, you know how bad it is."

No, the girl who was leaning on the fence had never been ha'nted, but her eyes were wide with pity for the old soul who had marched through Georgia and forgotten the tune.

"Some days I 'most ketch it. I don't suppose"—the old voice halted diffidently—"I don't suppose you'd whistle it, would you? Jest through once—"

But she could not whistle even once "Through Georgia." "I'm so sorry!" she cried. "I can't whistle, or sing, or anything. I wish I could!" She wished she were Billy; Billy could have done it.

Old '61 marched on, up the dusty road, and the girl went back to her tree. She had not sold any daisy-handkerchiefs, but she had her story to tell the girls. She lay in the grass thinking of it. Once or twice she pursed her lips and made a ludicrous ineffectual attempt to whistle, but she did not smile. Jane Cotton's Sam clicked the gate, going out, but she did not notice. When she did at last look up, and her gaze wandered over the little yard aimlessly, she suddenly uttered a little note of surprise.

"Why!" she cried.

CHAPTER IV.

For the pump was a blue pump! A miracle had been wrought while she mused in the grass and listened to Old '61. The little old brown pump had blossomed out gayly, brilliantly.

"Why!" Then a subdued chuckle reached her from some nearby ambush out beyond the fence. She put two and two together—the pump, the laugh, and Jane Cotton's Sam. Six! Jane Cotton's Sam, while she was day-dreaming and Marching through Georgia with Old '61, had painted the brown pump blue! That was his business on Mrs. Camp's premises. Mrs Camp had remembered—the dear, oh, the dear!—that she wanted a blue pump, and had got the boy to come and make one. And now, down behind the fence somewhere, the boy was laughing at her amazement. Well, let him laugh—she laughed, too! Suddenly she began to clap her hands by way of applause to her hidden audience.

The pump itself was distinctly a disappointment. In gay-hued pictures, seen by childish eyes, blue pumps accord with green grass and trees—in nature, seen by maturer eyes, there is something wrong with the colors. They look out of place—either the green growing things or the gay blue pump do not belong there. The girl's loyalty to little, kind Emmeline Camp would not let her admit that it was the blue pump that didn't "belong." She was glad—glad—that it was blue, for it stood for a thoughtful kindness to her, and thoughtful kindnesses had been rare in her self-dependent, hustling life.

"Hurrah for the blue pump!" she cried softly. She felt like going up to it and hugging it, but fortunately she did not yield to the impulse.

The other girls arrived at dusk. T.O., her knee in a chair, had hitched laboriously from little kitchen to little dining-room and got supper. Spent and triumphant, she waited in the doorway. She could hear their voices coming up the road—Billy's excited voice, Laura Ann's gay one, Loraine's calm and sweet. She longed to run out to meet them. Next best, she sent her own voice, in a clear, long call.

"That's T.O.! Girls, let's run!" she heard Billy say.

"Why doesn't she run?" Laura Ann demanded severely. "That would be perfectly appropriate under the circumstances."

"'Tis queer, isn't it, that she didn't come to meet us?" Loraine added. In another moment they had reached Emmeline Camp's little green-painted house and found the Talented One waiting impatiently at the gate. Things explained themselves rapidly. Exclamations of pity crowded upon exclamations of delight and welcome. Four happy young wage-earners sat down to T.O.'s hardly-prepared little supper and four tongues were loosed. Even Loraine did her part of the chattering.

"I feel so nice and placid already!" enthused Billy.

"Oh, so do I!—so do I!" echoed Laura Ann. "It's such a comfort to get one's chains off!—I felt mine slip off back there at that dear, funny little station."

"Oh, was that what I heard clanking?" offered quiet Loraine, and was promptly cheered.

The meal was a merry one. And afterwards there was exploring to be done about the little yard and orchard and up and down the road, in the dim, sweet twilight, with the Talented One at the gate calling soft directions.

"And I've got a blue pump for you," she laughed. "Just wait till daylight! Don't anybody feel of it in the dark to see if it's blue, because you'll find it's green! There's a story goes with the pump and one with its mother—I mean with the boy-who-painted-its mother! Placid Pond is full of stories."

"Nice, dozy, placid ones, I suppose," Laura Ann returned lightly. But the Talented One shook her head.

"Wait till you hear them," she said gravely.

"Give us some of the titles to-night," coaxed Billy. They were all back on the little doorsteps and the moon was rising, majestic and golden, behind the trees.

"Well—" she considered thoughtfully, "there's 'The Story of Amelia', and the story of 'The Boy Who Didn't Pass', and the one of 'Old '61'—",

"Oh, tell us—tell us!" Billy pleaded, and would not be refused. It was never easy to refuse Billy. She had her way this time, and there in the mellow night-light, with soft night-noises all about them, T.O. told her stories. She had never told a story before in her life, and her voice at first stumbled diffidently, but as she went on, a queer thing happened—she did not seem to be telling it herself, but the little old woman who loved Amelia seemed to be telling it! Then the Boy Who Didn't Pass, then Old '61, in his tremulous, halting old voice.

They listened in perfect silence, and even after the stories ended they said nothing. Billy, quite unashamed, was crying over poor Old '61.

"You'd have thought, wouldn't you," T.O. murmured after a while, "that places like this would be humdrum-y and commonplace? But I guess there are 'stories' everywhere. I'm beginning to find out things, girls."

The next day began in earnest the long-yearned-for time of rest. It was decided unanimously over the breakfast cups, to live and move, eat and all but sleep, out of doors. To devote four separate and four combined energies to having a good time. To abide by the rules and regulations of the Wicked Compact—long live the Wicked Compact! Laura Ann made an illuminated copy of it, framed it in a border of hurriedly-painted forget-me-nots and hung it on the screen door, where they could not help seeing it and "remembering their vows," Laura Ann said. It was a matter of gay conjecture with them who would be the first to break the Compact.

"And be driven out of the B-Hive—not I!" Billy said decisively. "I shan't have the least temptation to break it, anyway—I feel selfish all over! You couldn't drive me to do a good deed with a—a pitchfork!"

"Me either—not even with a darning-needle!" laughed Laura Ann. "If anybody asks me to lend her a pin, hear me say, 'Can't, my dear; it's against the rules.' Needn't anybody worry about losing me out o' the Hive!"

"Loraine will be the one—you see," T.O. said lazily. "And what I want to know is, how are we going to live without Loraine? I vote we append a by-law. By-law I.: 'Resolved, that we except Loraine—just Loraine.'"

"Second the motion," murmured Billy, on her back in the grass, nibbling clover heads.

"No," Loraine said severely, "I refuse to be put into a by-law."

The summer days were long days—lazy, somnolent days. The four girls spent them each in her own separate way. Sometimes the little colony met only at mealtimes—with glowing reports of the mornings' or afternoons' wanderings.

Billy, it was noticed, although like the rest she wandered abroad, made no reports. Had she had a good time? Yes—yes, of course. Where had she been all the morning or all the afternoon? Oh—oh, to places. Woods? Yes—that is, almost woods. And more than that they failed to elicit. Nearly every day she started away by herself, and after awhile they noticed that she went in the same direction. She went briskly, alertly, like one with a definite end in view. Now, where did Billy go? Their vagrant curiosity was aroused, but not yet to the point of investigation.

Old '61 knew. Every morning since that first morning he had strained his dim old eyes to catch a glimpse of a little figure coming blithely up the road. On that first morning it had stopped in front of his little house and said pleasant things to him as he sat on the doorsteps. He remembered all the things.

"Good-morning! It's a splendid day, isn't it?"

And: "What a perfectly lovely place you live in! With the woods so near you can shake hands with them out of your windows!"

And: "Don't the birds wake you up mornings? I wonder what they sing about up here." Then she had glanced at his ancient army coat and added the Pleasantest Thing Of All: "I think they must sing Battle Hymns and Red, White and Blue songs and 'Marching Through Georgia,' don't they?"

"Not the last one," he had answered sadly. "They never sing that. If they did, I'd 'a' learnt it of 'em long ago."

"Do you like that one best—very best?" she had asked, and he liked to remember how she had smiled. He had stood up then and thrown back his old shoulders proudly.

"Why, you see, marm," he had said simply, "I marched through Georgy!"

The next morning, too, she had stopped and talked to him. But it was not until the third time that he had ventured to ask her to whistle it. And then—Old '61, now peering down the road for the blithe little figure, thrilled again at the remembrance of what had happened. She had laughed gently and said she did not know how to whistle, but if he would like her to sing it—

There had been eight mornings all told, now, counting this morning, which was sure to be. Yes, clear 'way down there somebody was comin' swingin' along—somebody little an' happy an' spry. Old '61 began to laugh softly. He could hardly wait for her to come and sit down on the doorstep and sing it. Two or three times—she would sing it two or three times.

He had a surprise for her this morning. With great pains he had dragged his cabinet organ out onto the little porch. It was all open, ready. He went a little way down the road in his eagerness to meet her.

"Good-morning!" Billy called brightly. "Am I late to-day?"

"Jest a little—jest a little," he quavered joyously, "but I'll forgive ye! There's somethin' waitin' up there—I've got a surprise for ye!"

"Honest?" Billy stood still in the road, looking into the eager, childish old face. "Oh, goody! I love surprises. Am I to guess it?"

"No, no, jest to come an' play on it!" he quavered. Then a cloud settled over his face and dimmed the delight in it. "Mebbe you don't know how to?" he added, a tremulous upward lift to his voice.

"How to 'play on' a surprise!" cried Billy. "Well, how am I to know until I see it? I can play on 'most everything else!"

They had got to the little front gate—were going up the little carefully-weeded path—were very close to it now. Billy sprang up the steps.

"I can! I can!" she laughed. "Hear me!" Her fingers ran up and down the keys, then settled into a soft, sweet little melody. Another and another—

The old man on the lower step sat patiently listening and waiting. If she did not play it soon, he should have to ask her to, but he would rather have her play it without. Perhaps the next one—

The next one was beautiful, but not It—not It—not the Right One.

"There!" finished Billy with a flourish. "You see, I can play on a surprise!" She stopped abruptly at sight of the disappointed old face below her. For an instant she was bewildered, then a beautiful instinct that had lain unused on some shelf of Billy's mind came to life and whispered to her what the trouble was.

"Oh!" she cried softly, "Oh, I'm sorry I forgot!" She turned back to the little organ and began to play again.

Up went the sagging old head, up the sagging old shoulders! Old '61 was back in "Georgy," marching through mud and pine-barrens, in cold and hunger and weariness—with the boys, from Atlanta to the sea. Hurrah! hurrah! the flag that made them free!

He was not old, not alone and forlorn and cumbering the earth. He was young and straight and loyal, defying suffering and death, with glory and fame, perhaps, on there ahead. His country needed him—he was marching through Georgia for his country.

Billy played it over and over, untiring. A lump grew in her throat at the sight of the old face down there on the lower step. For so much was written on the old face!

Suddenly Old '61 got up and began to march, swinging his old legs out splendidly. Down the walk, down the road, he went, as far as the music went, then came marching splendidly back.

Head up, shoulders squared, the "boys" marching invisible beside him and before him and behind him, he was no longer Old '61, but Young '61.

The next day Billy ate her breakfast quietly, helped clear away the things, and went quietly away. She did not stop to read Laura Ann's gay-painted "Compact" on the screen door. It might even have been noticed, if anyone cared to notice, that she did not look at it, that she hurried a little through the door, as if to avoid it.

Old '61 was waiting at the gate. She smiled at the eager invitation she read in his face.

"No," she said, shaking her head for emphasis, "no, I'm not going to play it this time. I'm going to teach you to play it! I shall be going back to the city before long, and then what will you do when you want to hear it? Perhaps you couldn't keep the tune in your head. I'm going to show you an easy way to play it—just the air. I shall have to try it myself first, of course. But I'm sure you can learn how, if you'll practice faithfully." It was queer how her music-teacher tone crept back into her voice. She laughed to herself to hear it. "Practice faithfully" sounded so natural to say!

She sat down at the organ and experimented thoughtfully, trying to reduce the old man's beloved tune to its very lowest terms. After quite a long time she nodded and smiled.

Then began Old '61s music lessons. It was terrible work, like earning a living with the sweat of the brow. But the two of them—the young woman and the old man—bent to it heroically. For an hour, that first time, the cramped old fingers felt their way over the keyboard; for an hour Billy bent over them, patiently pointing the way. She had forgotten that she was not to think of piano-notes now—that she had signed the Wicked Compact. She had forgotten everything but her determination to teach Old '61 to play "Marching through Georgia." And Old '61 had, in his turn, forgotten things—that he was old, alone, a cumberer, everything but his determination to learn It.

It was not a scientific lesson. It did not begin with first principles and creep slowly upward; it began in the middle, in a splendid, haphazard, ambitious way. The stiff old hands were gently placed in position for the first notes of the tune, the stiff old fingers were pressed gently down, one at a time. Over and over and over the process was repeated. It was learning by sheer brute patience and love.

"That's all for the first lesson," Billy announced at the end of the hour. "You've got those first notes well enough to practice them. To-morrow we'll go a little bit farther." But she did not know the long, patient hours between now and then that the old man would "practice," crooked painfully over the keys. She did not reckon on the miracle that might be wrought out of intense desire.

The next morning Old '61 at the gate proclaimed proudly:

"I've got it! I've got it! I can play an' sing fur as we've b'en! It's ringin' in my head all the time."

"Did the birds wake you up singing it?" Billy asked, smilingly. She, herself, was all eagerness to learn of her pupil's progress. The lesson began at once. Already, she found, the miracle had begun to work. The old man sat down to the organ with a flourish that, if it had not been full of pathos, would have been a little comedy act. After a brief preliminary search the old fingers found their place and pounded out triumphantly the few notes they had been taught.

"Good! good!" applauded the teacher heartily. "Why, you do it splendidly! Now we'll go on a little farther—this finger on this note, this one here, your thumb here." She stationed them carefully and the second lesson began. It was nearer two hours than one when it ended.

"Where have you been, Billy?" Loraine asked at lunch. They had all been describing their individual pursuits and experiences of the morning.

"Oh, to a place," answered Billy lightly.

"What place?" Loraine persisted curiously.

"Well," laughed Billy, "if you must know, I've been marching through—oh, a place!" she concluded hastily, repenting herself. "It was a pretty hard place, and I'm hungry as a bear. Wish somebody'd say, 'Won't you have another piece of pie?'"

"Won't you have another piece of pie?" laughed Loraine, and nothing further was said of an embarrassing nature.

The summer days grew into summer weeks. Patiently and joyously Old '61 plodded his way to the sea. He practiced nearly all his waking hours, and when he was not at the little organ, practicing, he went about humming the beloved words. Pride and love, rather than any melody of his cracked old voice, made a tune of them.

His progress astonished his teacher. Her praise was impetuous enough for further and greater exertions. One day Billy said the next time should be an exhibition, when he should play it all—from "Atlanta to the sea"—with her as audience, not helping, but sitting in a chair listening.

She came to the Exhibition in a white dress, with sweet-peas at her waist. Her smiles at the foot of the steps changed to something like a sob when she discovered that Old '61 had been decorating the organ and the little porch. He, himself, was brushed and radiant, his old face the face of a little child.

"The audience will sit on the steps," Billy said, a little tremulously. "Right here. Make believe I'm rows and rows of people! Now will you please favor us by 'Marching through Georgia'?".

He went at once to the little gayly-bedecked instrument and began to play. The dignity and pride of the shabby old figure redeemed its shabbiness—the fervor of the pounded notes redeemed the tune. The audience—in "rows and rows,"—listened gravely, and at the end burst into genuine applause. The sound swelled and multiplied oddly, and then they saw the three figures at the gate who had listened, too. Billy was discovered!

CHAPTER V.

They escorted Billy home. It was rather a silent walk until the end. Loraine spoke first.

"One less in the B-Hive," she said sadly.

"Yes, I suppose I'm dropped now," responded Billy, not uncheerfully. "Of course I've got to take the consequences of my—my crime. But I don't care!" she added with vivacity. "I'd rather live alone in a ten-story house than have missed that Exhibition!"

"Yes," mused Laura Ann thoughtfully, "it was a beautiful one. I'm glad I didn't miss it. When I think of what it stood for—"

She broke off suddenly and slipped her hand into Billy's arm. Another short silence. Then Laura Ann finished: "All the work and patience it stood for, day after day—girls, when I think of that I feel—"

"I know—all of us know," T.O. hastily interposed. "That's about the way we all feel, I guess. No use talking about it, though. Billy's broken the Compact and we're under oath to drop her."

"Not till we go back to work," Loraine put in emphatically, "and then she can live next door and come in every night to tea! There's nothing in the Compact against that, is there? Well, then, I invite you, Billy, for the very first tea!"

"I accept!" laughed Billy. She did not seem at all depressed. In her ears rang the pounding refrain of Old '61 marching through Georgia.

Nothing more was said on this subject. A little picnic had been planned for the afternoon, and they went briskly about making preparations for it, as soon as they got back to Mrs. Camp's little green house. While they worked they discussed Amelia.

"If she hadn't gone with her mother we'd have taken her to the picnic with us," the Talented One said, over her egg-beating. "I wonder if Amelia likes picnics?"

"Don't! You make me feel creepy," Laura Ann laughed. "What I wonder is how she'd have looked if she'd ever been born. I lay awake one night trying to imagine Amelia."

"Blue eyes and golden hair," Loraine chimed in dreamily, "and a little dimple in her chin."

"You needn't any of you lie awake nights imagining. I can tell you," the Talented One said. "She has blue eyes, but her hair is brown and the dimples are in her cheeks. Her hair just waves a little away from the parting—it is always parted. She sits very still, sewing patchwork—her mother told me," added the Talented One quietly. "She said she wished she knew how to paint so she could paint Amelia's picture. She told me where she'd like to have it hung—here in the dining-room, between the windows. Amelia'd always been very real, she said, but the picture would make her realer."

"Did she ever say what kind of dresses Amelia wears?" asked Laura Ann without looking up from her stirring.

"No, I never asked, but they must be white dresses, I think,—Amelia is such an innocent little thing," laughed T.O. softly. It was odd how they always laughed or talked softly when it was about little make-believe Amelia.

The picnic was in the woods, in a lovely little spot Loraine had discovered in her wanderings. A brook babbled noisily through the spot. They spread their lunch at the foot of a forest giant and ate it luxuriously to the tune the brook sang. It was hard to believe they had ever been toilers in a great city.

"There never were any public schools," murmured Loraine, lying back and gazing into the thick mesh of leaves overhead. "Nobody ever said 'Teacher! Teacher!' to me."

"There never were any negatives to be 'touched up'—nobody ever had their pictures taken," Laura Ann murmured, dreamy, too. "I've always been here beside this brook, lying on my back—what a beautiful world it's always been!"

The Talented One sat rigidly straight. "There have always been handkerchiefs," she sighed, "and there always will be. I shall have to go back there and sell them. When I look at all these leaves, it reminds me—there are leaves on handkerchiefs, straggling round the borders—ugh!"

It was foolish talk, perhaps, but it was the place and the time for foolish talk. After a little more of it they drifted apart, wandering this way and that in a delightful, aimless way. So little of their four lives had been aimless or especially delightful that they reveled in the sweet opportunity. Loraine wandered farthest. She came after awhile to a clearing where a small pond glimmered redly with the parting rays of the sun. A great boy lounged beside the pond dangling a pole. Loraine recognized him as Jane Cotton's Sam.

"Oh!" she said, "now I've made a noise and scared away your fish!"

"Ain't any fish," muttered the boy. He did not turn around. The pole slanted further and further, till it lay on the bank beside the boy.

"Oh, maybe there are, if you wait long enough—and nobody comes crashing through the bushes! I don't suppose—I mean if you are not going to use it any more yourself—" Loraine looked toward the idle pole. "I never fished in my life," she explained. The boy understood with remarkable quickness.

"You mean you'd like to try it?" he asked, and this time turned round. It was not at all a bad face on close inspection, Loraine decided. The veil of sullenness had lifted a little.

"Oh, but I just would! Only if I should have an accident and catch anything, whatever would I do! They—they are always cold and clammy, aren't they?"

Jane Cotton's Sam laughed outright, and Loraine decided that it was a very good face.

"I'll 'tend to all you catch," the boy said. He was busily baiting the hook; now he extended the pole to her.

"Wiggle it—up and down a little, like this," he directed, "and don't make any more noise than you can help. If you feel a bite, let me know."

"But I don't see how I can feel a bite unless they bite me—"

Again the boy laughed wholesomely. They were getting acquainted. The fishing began, and for what seemed to her a long time Loraine sat absolutely still, dangling the pole. Nothing happened for a discouraging while. Then Loraine whispered: "I feel a bite, but it's on my wrist! If it's a mosquito I wish you would 'shoo' it off."

Another wait. Then a real bite in the right place. In another moment Loraine landed a wriggling little fish in the grass. She did not squeal nor shudder, but sat regarding it with gentle pride.

"Poor little thing! I suppose I ought to put you back, but you're my first and only fish, and I've got to carry you home for the girls to see. You'll have to forgive me this time!" She turned to the boy. "I suppose he ought to be dressed, or undressed, or something, before he's fried, oughtn't he? I thought I'd like to fry him for breakfast, to surprise the girls—"

"I'll dress him for you," Jane Cotton's Sam said eagerly, "and bring him over in the morning in plenty o' time."

"Thank you," Loraine said heartily. "Now you'll have to let me do something for you. 'Turn about is fair play.' Couldn't I—" She hesitated, looking out over the still reddened water rather than at the boy's face. "Couldn't I help you in some way with your studies? That's my business, you know. It would really be doing me a kindness, for I may get all out of practice unless I teach somebody something!" Had Loraine, too, forgotten the Compact on the screen door?

The boy fidgeted, then burst out angrily: "I s'pose they've all been telling you I failed up in my exams? They have, haven't they? You knew it, didn't you?"

"Yes," Loraine answered quietly. "But I've heard a good many worse things in my life. I've heard of boys that smoked and drank and—and stole. What does missing a few examinations amount to beside things like those?" But the boy did not seem to have been listening to anything except his own angry thoughts. All his sun-browned young face was flooded with red; he had run his fingers through his hair till it stood up fiercely.

"They needn't trouble themselves 'bout me, nor you needn't, nor anybody needn't!" he declaimed loudly. "Anybody'd think they were saints themselves!"

"And I was a saint and everybody was saints!" laughed Loraine softly. But Jane Cotton's Sam did not laugh. He went striding away into the woods, his head flung up high. Loraine and the little dead fish were left behind. Oddly the girl was not thinking of the boy's rudeness in return for her kind offer of help, but of the flash of spirit in his eyes. It augured well for him, she was thinking, for spirit was spirit, although "gone wrong." In the right place, it should spur him on to a second attempt to get into college. What if she were to persist in her offer—were to work with him, urge him to work with her?

But he had chosen to spurn her advances. She shook her head sadly. On his own head be it. She turned her attention to the little dead fish.

"You poor dear, you look so dead and forlorn—what am I going to do with you? Someway you've got to go home with me and be fried." She took him up gingerly, but dropped him again—he was so slippery and damp! Wrap him in her handkerchief? But she had no pocket and she could never, never carry him in her sleeve which she had adopted as a pocket. So then she must leave him, must she? Poor little useless sacrifice!

Back at the picnic spot the girls were waiting for her. They went home in the late, sweet twilight.

A letter was tucked under the screen door where some friendly neighbor had left it. "Miss Thomasia O. Brown," Billy read aloud, and waved the letter in triumph, for the secret was out. The 'T' in T.O. stood for Thomasia!

"Well?" bristled the Talented One, "it had to stand for something, didn't it? It's awful, I know, but I'm not to blame—I didn't name myself, did I? I wish people could," she added with a sigh.

"Is it for a Thomas?" questioned Laura Ann curiously.

Thomasia nodded: "There was always a Thomas in the family until they got to me. They did the best they could to make me one." She was opening the letter with careful precision. "Why, of course, it's from Mrs. Camp!" she cried delightedly.

"My dear, I hope you are well and your friends have come, and Jane Cotton's Sam has not forgotten to paint the pump. I arrived here safely after a very long journey—my dear, I never dreamed the world was so big! This part of it is well enough, but give me Placid Pond! Now I am going to tell you something, and you may laugh all you're a mind to—I sha'n't hear! What I'm going to tell is, Amelia came, too. After I'd got good and settled down on the cars I looked up and knew she was sitting right opposite, on the seat I'd turned over. She seemed there—and you may laugh, my dear. I laughed, I was so pleased to have Amelia along. John doesn't know she came—Amelia never makes a mite of trouble! But everywhere I go she goes, my dear. I shouldn't tell you if I didn't feel you'd understand. If he hasn't painted it yet, the blue paint is on a shelf in the woodhouse, and you can paint it. I'm afraid Jane Cotton's Sam won't ever amount to much. Poor Jane!"

Thomasia read the letter aloud, and at this point Loraine interposed warmly: "Jane Cotton's Sam is abused! It's a shame everybody groans over him—I like him. If there isn't a lot of good in him, then I don't know how to read human nature, that's all."

The next morning very early someone knocked at the kitchen door. It was Laura Ann's turn to make the fire, and she answered the knock. Jane Cotton's Sam stood on the steps outside. He had a mysterious little package in his hand. He looked up eagerly, but it was evident from the disappointed look on his face that Laura Ann was the wrong girl. And he did not know the right one's name!

"Good-morning!" nodded Laura Ann, sublimely unconscious of the soot-patch over her nose.

"Good-morning. I'd like to see—I've brought something for the one that teaches school."

"Loraine? But she isn't up yet—"

"Yes, I am up, too," called a voice overhead, "but I won't be long! I'll be down."

It was a little fish, dressed and ready to fry, that was in the tiny bundle. The boy extended it blushingly. Then his eyes lifted to Loraine's in frank petition for pardon.

"I was mighty rude," he said. "I went back to the pond to say so, but you were gone. I beg your pardon."

She liked the tone of his voice and his good red blushes. "That's all right," she nodded reassuringly. But he did not go away. There was something else.

"If—you know what you said? If you'd offer again—"

Loraine glanced over her shoulder. Laura Ann was rattling stove-lids at the other end of the kitchen. "I offer now," Loraine said in a low voice.

"Then I accept." The boy's voice was eager. "I'll study like everything! I thought about it in the night—I thought I'd like to surprise my mother. If I could get into college next year—" His eyes shone. "Oh I say, I'd do 'most anything for that!"

The little plan was hurriedly made, in low tones, there on Emmeline Camp's little doorsteps. The boy was to take his books to the pond where Loraine had caught her fish. He was to study there alone for a time every day, and in the afternoon she was to stroll that way and go over the work with him and set him right in all the wrong places.

"It was in Latin and mathematics I failed up," Jane Cotton's Sam explained.

"It's Latin and mathematics we'll tackle!" softly laughed Loraine. "You wait—you see—you grind!"

He strode away, whistling, and the tune was full of courage and determination. Loraine smiled as she listened. She stood a moment, then opened the screen door and went in. The "Compact" swung and tilted with the jolt of her energetic movements. She adjusted it with a queer little smile.

For summer days on summer days the covert, earnest lessons went on beside the bit of sunny water. Teacher and pupil pored intently over the problems and difficult passages, and steadily the pupil's courage grew. The old sullen look had vanished—Jane Cotton's Sam put on manliness and a splendid swing to his shoulders. In her heart Loraine exulted. What if she were disobeying the Compact—death to the Wicked Compact!

Laura Ann suspected, but for reasons of her own kept her own counsel. She had begun to suspect, when Jane Cotton's Sam brought the little fish. At that time the "reasons of her own" had begun to influence her and she had omitted to mention to Billy and T.O. that the boy had stood on the doorsteps in earnest conversation with Loraine. Mentioning it to Billy might not, indeed, have mattered, since Billy was already an "outsider." But Loraine might not want T.O. to know, anyway.

It was significant that Laura Ann, in going in and out, now chose to ignore the gayly-illuminated placard that swung on the door—that she herself had adorned and hung there. But she did not go in and out as much now; for whole mornings she slipped away to a little attic room upstairs and busied herself alone.

It was getting grievously near the time to go back to the great city again. Emmeline Camp was coming back then.

All but T.O. mourned audibly the rapidly lessening days, but T.O. made no useless laments. One day she surprised them.

"Girls, I want to go back!" she announced. "I shall be ready when it's time—now anybody can say what anybody pleases. Scoff at me—do. I expect it! But I'm getting homesick to see a street-car and a—a policeman! It's lovely and peaceful here, but I've had my fill of it now—I want to go home and bump into crowds and hear big, stirry noises. It's different with you girls—you weren't born in the city; you didn't play with street-cars and policemen and get sung to sleep by the noises! I was tired—tired—and now I'm rested. I've had a perfectly beautiful time, but I shall be ready to go back. Honestly, girls, it would break my heart not to!"

It was so much like T.O., Billy said, to keep all her feelings to herself and then suddenly spring them on people like that, and take people's breath away. Billy did not keep things to herself.

Jane Cotton came up the kitchen path one day when all but Loraine were sitting on the doorsteps—Loraine had strolled nonchalantly down the street as her afternoon habit was.

"Well, I've found out!" announced Jane Cotton. She was beaming; her sallow face was oddly cleared and lighted—her lips trembled with eagerness to deliver her news. "I've found out! Where's the rest o' you?" She counted them over. "It's the rest o' you I want—well, you tell her I've found out. Tell her I hardly slept a wink last night, I was so happy! Tell her Ibless her, and I know the Lord will. They didn't want me to know yet but I couldn't help finding out. And they won't mind when they know how happy it's made me—oh, I ain't afraid but he'll pass this time! I know he will—I know it! You tell her she's saved my boy." And without further delay the slender figure turned and walked jubilantly down the path. It was as if she marched to the melody of the joy in her heart.

They looked at each other silently, then at the Wicked Compact behind them. There did not seem any explanation needed.

"Another one dropped," murmured T.O. sighingly. But Laura Ann said nothing.

CHAPTER VI.

Laura Ann stole quietly away and went upstairs to the little attic room. Close by the window was a rough little easel arrangement with a picture on it. Laura Ann stood regarding it thoughtfully. "I wonder"—she smiled at the whimsy of the thought—"I wonder if it looks like Amelia," she murmured.

It was not a wonderful picture. No committee would have hung it on a "line." There were rather glaring errors in it of draughtsmanship and coloring. But the face of the girl in it was appealingly sweet—brown hair, blue eyes, little round chin. Laura Ann had not dared to put in the dimples.

"Dimples need a master," she said, "besides, they only show when you smile, and I don't believe Amelia smiles very often!"

She sat down and took up a brush. The picture was nearly done, but she found touches to be added here and there. There might be a stray lock—there, like that. And a little bit more shade under the chin, and the wistful droop of the mouth relieved, oh, a very little bit! Amelia looked so serious.

"Poor little thing! Well, it's a serious matter to be a dream-child, with not an ounce of good red blood in your veins."

Laura Ann meant to slip back after they had started for the station, on the last day, and hang the picture in the little sunny dining-room. She did not want the girls to know there was a picture. But still—a new thought had begun to obtrude itself unwelcomely. Was painting Amelia's portrait a breach, too, of the Compact? She had undertaken it as a little "offering" to Mrs. Camp, to show her own individual gratitude for her own share of the dear little green cottage all these beautiful weeks—T.O. had said Mrs. Camp had longed for a picture. But the fact that it had taken many patient hours of work "unto others," was not to be overlooked. If it had broken the rules of the Wicked Compact, and she went back to the B-Hive without letting the girls know of it—oh, hum! of course that would be another "wicked compact"! She would have to let them know—and she didn't want to let them know—oh, dear!

Suddenly Laura Ann dropped her paints and gave herself up to laughter. She had remembered that only T.O.—Thomasia O.—would be left now in the B-Hive! For all the rest had broken the Compact. Thomasia O., living all alone in the dear, shabby little rooms, presented a funny picture, for of them all she was least fitted to live alone. Even Billy could do better.

"The rest of us will live together," laughed Laura Ann. "There's nothing to prevent that, if we live outside the old B-Hive. We'll start a new B-Hive! Poor Thomasia O.!"

They would miss T.O. very much indeed—well, they could invite her in to tea and keep her all night! In spite of the wicked old Compact, they would keep together. "And we'll never," vowed Laura Ann for them all, "sign any more nefarious bonds!"

She hung the picture of Amelia on the wall when they were all away, and then went away herself. She stayed away until nearly dark. Thomasia O. went to meet her.

"I knew it all the time," she said quietly, without preface of any kind. "It's a perfect likeness."

"You knew it?" said Laura Ann.

"Yes, I was prowling 'round one day, to see what attics were like, and I found Amelia. Only her hair and her eyes, then, but I knew her. I'm so glad poor Mrs. Camp will have that picture to help her bear her troubles!"

"Poor"—"troubles." This was all enigma to Laura Ann. But she wisely waited to be enlightened. She had divined the moment she saw T.O. that the girl was unusually disturbed. This was true.

"I've had two letters—the first one came three weeks ago from her brother. I didn't want to spoil your good time, telling sad things, so I kept it to myself—Laura Ann, that womanmothered me!"

Laura Ann stood still. "Do you mean Mrs. Camp? Is she—dead?" But the other did not seem to hear. She ran on in a low, troubled voice.

"She bathed my ankle, and said 'My dear,' and waited on me, when she'd never set eyes on me in her life before. How did she know but that I was an—an impostor? And she let us have her dear little house to live in—"

"Yes, yes—oh, yes, she let me live in it!" Laura Ann interposed. "You ought to have told us she was dead."

"She isn't dead. She's fallen downstairs and broken her hip. The doctor says it's so bad she won't ever walk again without crutches, her brother wrote. He said he wanted her to stay and live with him, but she wouldn't listen to it. She wanted to come home as soon as she possibly could. So she's coming—he's coming with her, to 'start' her."

T.O. fingered a letter in her hand in a nervous, undecided way, as if she were half inclined to read it to the other girl. It was not Emmeline Camp's brother's letter. It had come ten days ago, and she herself knew it by heart. How many, many times she had read it! She had cried over the wistful cry in it, and over Amelia's death—for the letter said that Amelia was dead.

"My dear," it said, "I've lost Amelia—you'd think she would have stood by her mother in her trouble, wouldn't you? But she hasn't been near me since. It seems queer—perhaps after people break their hips they can't 'feel' anything else but their hips! Perhaps it breaks their imaginations. Anyway, Amelia's dead, my dear. Sometimes I think mebbe I'd ought to be, too—a lone little woman like me, without a chick or a child. Old women with children can afford to tumble downstairs, but not my kind of old women. John is real good. He wants me to stay here, but I can't—I can't, I can't, my dear! I've got to be where I can limp out to the old pump and the gate and the orchard, on my crutches—I've got to see the old hills I was born in, and Old '61 marching past the house, and the old neighbors—I've got to die at home, my dear. So John can't keep me. I wish I was going to find you there. I keep thinking how beautiful it would be. You'd be out to the gate waiting, the way people's daughters wait for them. And mebbe you'd have the kettle all hot and we'd have a cup of tea together just as if I was the mother and you was—Amelia! All the way home I should be thinking about your being there. It's queer, isn't it, you went limping in that gate first, and now it's me? A good many things are queer, and some are kind of desolate. I've decided, my dear, that daughters have to be the kind that are born, to stay by a body in trouble. They have to be made of flesh and blood, my dear—and Amelia wasn't!

"I've written this a little to a time, laying on my back. Mebbe you won't ever read it. Mebbe I won't ever see you again, but you will remember, my dear, that I've loved you ever since I took off your stocking and saw your poor, sprained ankle. If the Lord would perform a miracle for me, I'd ask for it to be the bringing of Amelia to life and finding her you."

T.O. did not show the letter to Laura Ann. She put it in her pocket again, and they walked home slowly, talking of Mrs. Camp's sad accident. At the supper table it was voted that they all write a joint letter of sympathy to her, and express, at the same time, their united and separate thanks for her kindness to them in lending them her home.

Loraine wrote the letter, Laura Ann copied it, they all signed it. Into cold pen-and-ink words they tried to diffuse warmth and gratitude and sympathy, but the result was not very satisfying, as such results rarely are. Still, it was all they could do. Billy and Laura Ann went off to mail it.

"Do you begin to feel lonesome?" laughed Loraine softly, as she and T.O. sat on the steps in the dark. "Thinking of being left all alone in the Hive, I mean? The rest of us begin to feel lonesome, thinking of being left out! We had a grist of good times all together, didn't we? Remember the little 'treats' when you always brought home olives, and Billy sage cheese? Laura Ann used to change about—sometimes eclairs, sometimes sauerkraut! Always sardines for me. Oh, do you remember the treat with a capital 'T,' when we had ice cream and angel cake? And Billy wanted to divide the hole so as not to waste anything—there, I don't believe you've heard a word I said!"

She had not, for she was not there. Loraine put out her hand in the darkness, but could not find her. She had slipped away unceremoniously.

She was down in the road, walking fast and hard. The battle was on again.

"I thought I had it all decided—I did have! Why do I have to decide it over again?" she was saying stormily to herself. "I said I'd do it, and I'm going to do it—what am I down here fighting in the dark for?" But still she fought on.

It was so still about her, and with all her girl's heart she longed for noise again—car-bells and rattling wheels and din of men's voices. There were such wide spaces all about, and she longed for narrow spaces—for rows on rows of houses and people coming and going. It was the city-blood in her asserting itself. She had had her breath of space and freedom and green, growing things, and exulted in it while it lasted. Now she pined for her native streets. But all the sympathy and gratitude in her went out to the little old woman who was coming home to a lonely home—whose one dream-child was dead.

No one had ever really needed her before—to be needed appealed to her strongly. And in the short time between her own coming to Placid Pond and the coming of the other girls, a bond of real affection had been established between Mrs. Camp and herself.

But hadn't she been over all this before? Long ago she had decided what to do. Now, suddenly, she wheeled in the dark road and went hurrying in the other direction. She would go back to Loraine on the doorstep, and laugh and talk. She had decided "for good."

The stars came trooping out, and she lifted her face to them with a new sense of peace. They were such friendly, twinkling little stars.

T.O. was humming a lilty little tune when she came up the path in the starlight and joined Loraine again on the doorstep.

The other two girls were coming slowly back from the little country post office, both to hurry and have the pleasant walk over. Billy had been saying nice things about the portrait of Amelia they had found hanging on the wall.

"It's a dear!" she said heartily. "I wish I could make a picture like that."

"You've made one a thousand times better!" cried Laura Ann. "I saw it this afternoon."

"Me—make a picture?" Billy's voice was incredulous. "I couldn't draw my breath straight!"

"It was a beautiful one. I stood still and looked at it. Your background was fine, dear—woods banked against a late afternoon sky, with bits of red light straggling through the branches, a little box of a house in the foreground, with patches of new shingles on the 'cover'; a crooked little front path, a funny little well, a little rosebush all a flame of color—"

"Mercy!" Billy's little triangle of a face put on alarm. Was Laura Ann losing her mind?

"But that—all that—was only the setting. The heart of the picture, dear, was an old man marching up and down the path—did I say it was a moving picture? He was whistling a tune in a wheezy way, and keeping step to it grandly. Once he seemed to lose a few notes; then he went into a little box of a house, and I heard an organ—"

"Oh!" breathed Billy, assured of the other's sanity, "you mean Old '61 practicing! That's the way he does—he's learning to march through Georgia without the organ, but he misses a step or two sometimes. That was the picture, was it?"

"It was a beautiful one," Laura Ann said softly. "You needn't tell me you can't paint, Billy! That's the kind of pictures we shall find hanging in the Great Picture Gallery."

They walked on for a little in silence, with only the piping chorus of the little night creatures in their ears. The sweet, cool damp was in their faces.

"Here we are at Jane Cotton's Sam's," Billy whispered by and by, to break the spell. She could not have told why she whispered.

"So we are. Billy, look, he's studying like a trooper! That boy is going to walk straight into college in September! Let's go straight home and hug Loraine—come on! Take hold of my hand, and we'll run."

"Wait—wait! Look, there's another of your pictures, Laura Ann!" Billy's lips were close to the other's ear; Billy was pointing. Into the little lighted room where Jane Cotton's Sam sat poring over a book, had come another figure. As they looked, it stopped beside the boy and bent over him.

"That's just the setting—all that," Laura Ann murmured. "The heart of the picture is her face, Billy!" For Jane Cotton's face was radiant.

The day at last came for their return to the city and to the work they were so much better able to do. The little, green-painted house was in spotless order to leave behind. As Mrs. Camp was to come the following day, they had filled the little pantry with food—not remarkably light cake or bread, not especially flaky piecrust, but everything flavored with sympathy and gratitude and good will.

"Go on, all of you; I'll catch up," Billy said, as they stood on the steps with the door locked behind them. "When you get out of sight I'm going to kiss the house good-by!"

"T.O. had better stay behind with you, to kiss the pump!" Loraine said. "Or we'll all stay—I guess we can all find something to kiss."

"Did anybody think to take down the Wicked Compact?" demanded Laura Ann suddenly. "It would be awful to leave that behind."

They were at the gate. T.O. stopped suddenly, pointing. What they saw was a tiny, tiny mound, rounded symmetrically. "There it lies—I buried it," T.O. said briefly, but added, "And let no one keep its grave green!" They looked at her a little curiously. Perhaps they were thinking that it might have been appropriate for her to take it home with her and hang it on the wall to keep her company in the lonely little B-Hive. But they only laughed and tramped on cheerfully to the station. They were a little late, and had to run the last of the way. The train was already in, and they scrambled aboard.

"Well, here we are leaving Eldorado!" sighed breathlessly Loraine.

"And all of us heart-broken but T.O.—girls, where's T.O.?"

She was not there. The train was getting under way. In a flurry they huddled to the windows.

"Good-by! Good-by!" shouted a gay voice from the platform. A little white envelope flew in at one of the open windows. T.O., quite calm and unexcited, stood out there waving to them.

"What in the world!" ejaculated Laura Ann, then stopped. For she alone could see a little ray of light. "Read the letter," she said more quietly. "The letter will tell us."

They all read it together, their heads bunched closely.

"Dear girls, I'm going to stay. I never was needed before, but I guess I am now. And maybe you'll think it's funny, but I'm wanted! An imaginary daughter can't wait on a poor little cripple—it takes the flesh-and-blood kind. I found out she wanted me, and so I'm going to stay. It would have been lonesome, anyway, all alone in the Hive! I bequeath all my rights to you—"

"As if she had any now, any more than the rest of us!" muttered Billy fiercely, her eyes full of tears.

"Sometimes when you're going and coming, some o' you listen to the car-wires sing, for me, and the wheels rattle," the letter went on. "Bump into somebody sometime for me! Good-by. You're all of you dears.

"Amelia."

At the signature they choked a little, and looked away at the flying landscape without seeing it at all. Laura Ann saw another picture—a girl waiting at a little gate. Woods and dusty road and humble little homes for background, and an old stage rattling into view in the foreground. She saw it stop—in the picture—and a helpless little old figure be taken out. She saw the girl at the gate spring forward and hold out her hands. But the heart of the picture was the face of the little old woman on crutches. It was another picture for the Grand Gallery.

9 781836 572525